Lullabyhullaballoo!

Mick Inkpen

ARTISTS & WRITERS GUILD BOOKS
Golden Books
Western Publishing Company, Inc.

The sun is down.
The moon is up.
It is bedtime for the
Little Princess.
But outside the castle…

A dragon is roaring.
What shall we do?
He's hissing and snorting!
What shall we do?
We'll tell him to SSSH!
That's what we'll do.

SSSH!

YES YOU!

But,

The brave knights are clanking.
What shall we do?
They're rattling and clunking!
What shall we do?
We'll tell them to SSSH!
That's what we'll do.

SSSH!

YES YOU!

But,

The ghosts are oooooing.

What shall we do?

They're ooo ooo oooooing!

What shall we do?

We'll tell them to SSSH!

That's what we'll do.

SSSH!

YES YOOOOOOOO!

But,

The giant is stamping.

What shall we do?

He's galumphing and stomping!

What shall we do?

We'll tell him to SSSH!

That's what we'll do.

SSSH!

Y ES DO!

But,
Out in the forest
    Wolves are howling

Owls are hooting
    Frogs are croaking

Mice are squeaking
    Bats are flapping

Bears are growling

And the trolls
and the goblins
are guzzling
and gobbling
and slurping
and burping!

What shall we do?

We'll tell them to...

...STOP!

But now,
The Princess is crying!
What shall we do?
She won't stop howling!
What shall we do?
We'll sing her a lullaby.
That's what we'll do.
We'll ALL sing a lullaby.

Now the Princess is smiling.

Her eyelids are drooping.

The Princess is sleeping.

So what shall we do?
We'll tiptoe to bed
And we shall sleep too.
We shall sleep too.

snore!
snore!
snore!
snore!
snore!
snore!
snore!
snore!

…the Princess is snoring!
What *shall* we do?

snore

snore!

snore!